The April Fool's Day Mystery

The April Fool's Day Mystery

Marion M. Markham

Illustrated by Pau Estrada

HOUGHTON MIFFLIN

Boston • Atlanta • Dallas • Geneva, Illinois • Palo Alto • Princeton

Library of Congress Cataloging-in-Publication Data

Markham, Marion M.
  The April Fool's Day mystery / Marion M. Markham : illustrated by
Pau Estrada.
     p.   cm.
  Summary: The Dixon twins try to discover who put the snake in the
school cafeteria flour bin on April Fool's Day, clearing an unjustly
suspected classmate in the process.
  ISBN 0-395-56235-X
  [1. Mystery and detective stories. 2. Twins—Fiction. 3. April
Fool's Day—Fiction. 4. Practical jokes—Fiction. 5. Snakes—
Fiction.] I. Estrada, Pau, ill. II. Title.
PZ7.M33946Ap   1991   90-41318
[Fic]—dc20   CIP
                     AC

Printed in The United States of America

123456789-WC-04 03 02 01 00 99 98

Contents

1

Puzzles and Pranks

On the first day of April, Kate Dixon measured the daffodils. Kate measured the daffodils every morning on her way to school. Daffodil growth was her new interest. Kate liked science, and she wanted to see if the growth was connected to the weather.

Her twin sister, Mickey, walked on without her. Mickey wasn't interested in daffodils. She wanted to be a detective. When she wasn't trying to solve mysteries, she was reading mystery stories.

In the schoolyard, the usual April First foolishness was going on. Someone tried to stick a sign on Suzy Kaminsky's back that said: SNOOZY SUZY. A sixth-grade boy dangled a black rubber spider on a

1

string in front of the girls' faces. When the girls screamed, he yelled, "April Fool." Most of the fifth-grade class was gathered around Billy Wade.

"When Mrs. Riley tells us to take out our arithmetic books," Billy said, "we'll all sit on the floor."

Debbie Allen said, "Why?"

"Because it's April Fool's Day."

"But why sit on the floor? It's dirty."

"All right," he said. "*We'll* sit on the floor. *You* stand up."

"I don't see what sitting on the floor has to do with April Fool's Day," Debbie insisted.

Mickey didn't quite see, either. She and Kate had already decided to trade desks and see how long it took Mrs. Riley to catch on.

Billy said, "The teachers expect us to do something." His voice squeaked in annoyance. "That was the only thing I could think of that wouldn't make Mrs. Riley angry. Do you have a better idea?"

"It's dumb," said Debbie. But no one could think of anything else to do. And it wasn't as dumb as some of Billy's tricks. Finally she said, "You have to yell 'April Fool' right away."

2

Mickey was already seated at Kate's desk when her twin slipped in just before the tardy bell. Angela Fergusen was even later. She dashed in as the bell stopped ringing. Usually, Mrs. Riley would have said something to the two stragglers.

Today, however, she said, "Everyone take out paper and pencil." Someone in the back of the room groaned. "Take out paper and pencil" meant they were getting a test.

The groans turned to giggles when she added, "Wouldn't you be more comfortable at your own place, Kate?"

The twins switched desks while Mrs. Riley raised the large map of the world. On the blackboard under the map were six questions.

Mickey read, "What is the highest grade you could get on this test?" A very weird first question. She wrote "100" as her answer.

Kate also thought the questions were weird. But easy. The second one said, "Name a green vegetable that grows inside a pod." Number three said, "Give the plural form of 'is.'" What a silly test! Mickey thought, before she realized it was Mrs. Riley's April Fool's joke.

After she answered the fourth question, "When we wink we close one _____," Mickey went back and changed her first answer for the highest grade from "100" to "A."

"A, pea, are, eye," she repeated silently in her head. The first four letters of April. Kate recognized them, too, and giggled.

Mrs. Riley looked at her sternly. Then she smiled and said, "I see that some of you are awake this morning."

Mickey had no trouble figuring out that an elevated train used for transportation in a city was an el. And, of course, another name for jesters and clowns — the sixth question — was fools. As she was writing her last answer, a loud scream echoed through the building.

Boys and girls jammed the classroom door.

"Children, sit down," Mrs. Riley said. She was no longer smiling. "Take out your arithmetic books and do the problems on page one hundred eighty-three."

Even Billy Wade was too surprised to sit on the floor. While the class did arithmetic, Mrs. Riley left the room. Normally, this would be a time when the girls whispered and the boys shot paper wads. But everyone was quiet. They were thinking about the terrified scream.

What had happened?

Who had screamed?

2

A Real Private Eye

When she returned, Mrs. Riley didn't explain until all the arithmetic papers had been turned in.

Then she said, "I'm sure you're wondering what happened."

Debbie Allen bobbed her head up and down so hard her hair bow fell out.

"Someone put a snake in the kitchen flour bin." Mrs. Riley paused and looked around the room as if searching out the guilty one. "When Mrs. Gateley opened the bin" — her eyes stopped at Billy Wade — "the snake slithered over her hand."

Mickey wondered if the snake was another one of Billy's tricks. But Kate's scientific curiosity bubbled up. What kind of snake was it?

Angela Fergusen shuddered and whispered loudly, "How awful." Obviously, Angela didn't like snakes.

Kate thought that was peculiar since Angela's brother collected snakes. But maybe that was *why* she didn't like them.

"Some April Fool's jokes aren't funny," Mrs. Riley continued. "When Mrs. Gately jumped back, she banged her head."

Billy asked, "Was she hurt?"

"Fortunately not," Mrs. Riley said. "But it could have been very serious."

7

She began erasing the test from the board. "Mr. Jacobi has banned all further celebration of April Fool's Day." Still holding the eraser, she faced the class again. "The jokes are over. If anyone tries anything, I'll send him — or her — to Mr. Jacobi's office."

Mickey looked at Billy. From his expression, she couldn't tell if he was guilty. But when there was trouble, he was usually responsible. Billy Wade spent a lot of time in the principal's office.

During recess, everyone talked about the snake in the flour bin. As usual, imaginations went crazy. The story — and the snake — grew and grew.

At lunch, the boy with the rubber spider was still scaring girls. Miss Heckler, the teacher on lunchroom duty, took away the spider and sent him to the office. There were shudders about another joke, too. Someone had put sugar in the salt shakers.

Angela Fergusen made a terrible face and said, "Disgusting," after tasting a sugary French fry.

Mostly, though, the talk was still about the snake. What had probably been a harmless garter snake turned into a king cobra planted by a foreign spy.

Kate knew that the only cobras in the United States lived in zoos. But this wasn't a day to be too smart about snakes. Not when everyone was suspicious of everyone else.

The twins were almost through eating when Billy Wade came over.

"I want to hire you," he said.

Kate said, "Didn't you hear Mrs. Riley say no more April Fool's jokes?"

"It's not a joke," Billy said. "I really want to hire you."

"What for?" said Mickey.

"Everyone thinks I put the snake in the flour," he said.

"Did you?" asked Kate.

"No." Billy was emphatic. "I like Mrs. Gately's pizzaburgers."

Thursday was pizzaburger day, and Mrs. Gately always baked the buns herself. Today no one ate any of them — not even after Mr. Jacobi announced that the flour hadn't come from the bin.

"Why do you want to hire us?" Mickey said.

Billy looked surprised. "Find out who did it so they'll stop blaming me." He looked at her. "You want to be a detective, don't you?"

Mickey raised her head and stuck out her chin. "I *am* a detective," she said. Then she added, "What about a retainer?"

"What's that?" Billy asked.

"It's the money you give a private detective when you hire her."

Billy took two quarters from his pocket. "This is all I have. Is that enough to get you to detect the real criminal?"

Kate looked skeptical. "You're sure you didn't do it?"

"If I was going to put something in the flour, it wouldn't be a snake. Imagine a frog jumping out, and flour splattering . . ." He got a dreamy look on his face and never finished the sentence.

"I ought to be able to wrap up the case this afternoon," Mickey said. She took the fifty cents.

After Billy left, she squealed, "My first case."

"We've solved mysteries before," Kate said.

"But we've never been paid before. This makes me a real private eye."

3

Sleuthing Snakes

"All right, Miss Private Eye," Kate said. "Where do we start?"

Mickey said, "You're the scientist. What do you know about snakes?"

"They're cold-blooded animals."

"So was the person who put one in the flour bin," Mickey said.

"I mean that snakes don't have thermostats inside to control their body heat the way we do."

"So?"

"They aren't very active when it's cold," said Kate.

"What does that mean?"

"The snake had to be in the bin long enough to get warm. If someone brought it in from outside

just before school started, it would still be too cold
to slither across Mrs. Gately's hand."

"Good thinking," Mickey said. "What else do
you know?"

"Not much."

Mickey said, "Then *you* start by finding out
more about snakes."

"How?" Kate asked.

"In the school library, of course."

"But this isn't our library day."

"Ask for a hall pass."

Kate thought about that for a moment. Then
she said, "I guess I could tell Miss Heckler about
the daffodils and say I want a book on weather."

"Great idea."

"What will you be doing?"

Mickey said, "Private eying — I mean, spying. Criminals like to brag about their crimes."

"No one's going to brag to you," Kate said. "Your talent for solving mysteries is like Billy's talent for causing trouble. Everyone knows about it."

"I might overhear something." She turned around. "Hey, Debbie, wait up," Mickey called and hurried outside.

Kate looked around the lunchroom. She wished that Mrs. Riley had lunchroom duty today. She hardly knew Miss Heckler. She sighed. She had to try.

"Pardon me," Kate said to the teacher. "I need to look something up in the library. I'm working on a science project about how much daffodils grow every day and if their growth has anything to do with the weather's being sunny, or cold, or rainy, and I measure them every morning on my way to school so —"

"What do you want?" Miss Heckler interrupted.

"A pass to the library so I can read about flowers and see if the growth of daffodils is related to —"

Somewhere behind Kate, a scuffle broke out.

14

Miss Heckler called, "Boys, stop that fighting."
Then she turned back to Kate and asked, "Who's
your teacher?"

"Mrs. Riley."

Miss Heckler scribbled a note and handed it to
Kate.

"Thank you," Kate said and dashed out of the
lunchroom.

4

Private Eying

Outside, Mickey steered Debbie toward a group of girls from their own class. They were jabbering about the snake.

"Billy Wade must have done it," Angela Fergusen was saying. "He's always doing something bad."

Carol Clark said, "So's Tim Winston. My sister's in his room and she says he's always in trouble."

"Either one of them might think a wriggling snake is funny," said Debbie.

"Tim Winston wouldn't do that," Angela said firmly. "He works in the kitchen and thinks Mrs. Gately is neat for a grownup. It was *definitely* Billy who put the snake in the bin."

Debbie said, "You're picking on Billy because he grabbed your jump rope yesterday."

Angela curled her lips into a pout. "He made me fall. I have a big sore spot on my leg. He's a mean boy who likes to see people get hurt."

Carol said, "If Billy did it, he's going to be in real trouble this time."

"Who cares," said Angela.

Debbie said, "I'm tired of talking about the stupid old snake." What she did want to talk about was her new dress. She began describing the ruffled skirt with pink velvet bows.

Mickey wasn't interested in pink velvet bows. She wandered toward the field, where most of the boys were playing dodge ball. When he saw her, Billy Wade left the game.

"Find out anything yet?" he asked.

Mickey said, "You're in an awfully big hurry."

"You would be, too, if Mr. Jacobi had it in for you. One more time in his office and I'll be suspended."

"Maybe you did do it," Mickey said.

He seemed surprised. "You're crazy. Why would I give you fifty cents to solve the mystery if I was guilty?"

"To take suspicion away from yourself."

Now he seemed angry. "All right, Mickey Dixon," he said. "Give me back my money."

"Don't get lumpy. I was just testing you."

One of the boys in the field called, "Hey, Wade. Are you playing dodge ball or not?"

"I'll give you until three o'clock," Billy told Mickey.

5

Caught in the Library

The corridor outside the lunchroom was deserted. But Kate had to walk past the principal's office to get to the library. She was sure that today Mr. Jacobi wouldn't want anyone wandering around. Not even someone with a hall pass and a good reason.

When she passed the office, Kate waved her hall pass at the secretary. Luckily, Mr. Jacobi wasn't there. He was probably looking for the guilty person, too.

The library was always empty during lunch period. Kate found several books about reptiles listed in the card catalogue. When she went to the shelf, she saw that most of them were about identifying snakes.

"Kate Dixon," a familiar voice said. Kate turned around. Mrs. Riley was standing right behind her.

"Miss Heckler said you were here," Mrs. Riley said. "What are you looking for?"

Since Kate was holding a book with a picture of an orange and black king snake on the cover, she couldn't talk about daffodils. She remembered the April Fool's Day quiz. Maybe Mrs. Riley was the kind of teacher who would understand.

"People are saying that Billy Wade put the snake in the flour."

"And he didn't?"

"He says he didn't. He hired Mickey and me to find out who did do it."

Mrs. Riley said, "Suppose you did find out. Would you tell anyone?"

Kate was silent for a moment. She thought she knew what Mrs. Riley meant.

"Tattling is when you tell a grownup," she finally said. "We're only going to tell Billy Wade."

"Then I guess you wouldn't tell me, even if I helped you."

"I guess not," said Kate.

Now Mrs. Riley was silent. Then she said, "Besides learning about snakes, what else would help?"

Kate knew exactly. "Mickey would like to see the scene of the crime," she said.

Mrs. Riley laughed. "Since Mr. Jacobi has already searched the kitchen, I suppose it would be all right to let you look around."

"I'd rather stay here," Kate said. "Mickey's better with detecting, and I'm better with science."

"All right," said Mrs. Riley. "But don't be late for class." Kate looked at the big clock on the wall. She still had ten minutes.

As she read, she thought she might as well have gone to the kitchen. She already knew that snakes didn't move much when they were cold. They were also lazy when they got hot, she learned. But that didn't matter. On April first, there was no way a snake would get too hot.

6

The Scene of the Crime

Mickey was discouraged. She hadn't found a single clue, and lunch would be over soon. Perhaps if she stood near the door when the bell rang, she might overhear something.

She was waiting at the entrance when Mrs. Riley stuck her head out.

"You want to look around the kitchen?" she said.

"Do I," Mickey said.

"Come on, then."

"How did you know?" Mickey asked.

"I saw Kate in the library."

Mickey didn't know if that meant they were in trouble. She was afraid to ask.

In the kitchen, Suzy Kaminsky and Tim Winston were working to earn lunch money. Tim was scraping food off plates, and Suzy loaded them into the dishwasher. They both looked up when Mrs. Riley and Mickey came in.

Mrs. Riley whispered something to Mrs. Gately, and the woman wiped her hands on her apron.

"Here's where I found the snake," she said. She opened a large can sitting next to the stove.

Mickey almost expected to see a forked tongue waving at her, but the can was empty.

"Mr. Jacobi took the snake outside. The flour went in the garbage," Mrs. Gately said.

Mickey asked, "What kind of snake was it?"

"A small blue racer," said Mrs. Gately. "Harmless, but very fast. Mr. Jacobi chased it all over the kitchen before it slithered under the stove."

Mickey smiled. She had a mental picture of the principal chasing the snake.

"Someone must have hidden it in the flour yesterday," she said.

"Why do you think that?" Mrs. Gately asked.

"A simple deduction," Mickey said. "It was cold last night. Kate said that if the snake had been outside, it would have been too cold to slither around."

Mrs. Riley smiled.

"Could anyone have gotten into the kitchen after school yesterday?" Mickey asked Mrs. Gately.

"I suppose so. I had a dentist's appointment and left early. The girls stayed to put the clean dishes away."

Mickey's detective instinct began tingling. She had her first real clue.

"Who locked up after them?" she asked.

Mrs. Gately said, "They were to tell Mr. Butterfield when they were done."

Mr. Butterfield was the school maintenance man. Almost everyone called him Mr. B.

Rrring echoed the bell announcing the end of lunch.

As they left the kitchen, Mrs. Riley said, "I suppose you want to talk to Mr. Butterfield."

Mickey was too surprised to answer. Could Mrs. Riley read minds? Billy Wade claimed she did. She remembered how quickly the teacher had realized that she and Kate had switched places this morning. The idea made her shiver.

Mrs. Riley continued. "I'll give you a pass to the boiler room during afternoon recess."

As Mickey and Mrs. Riley walked into the classroom, Kate and Billy Wade looked hopeful. Mickey shook her head and took out her English book.

7

What Mr. Butterfield Knows

Mickey decided that she and Kate would have to split up again at recess.

"I'll question Mr. B.," she whispered to her twin. "You talk to Suzy Kaminsky."

The maintenance man had a small office next to the boiler room. When Mickey came in, he put down the thick book he was reading. The red bow tie and yellow dress shirt he wore looked strange with his overalls. Maybe that was his April Fool's Day joke.

He said, "Tell your teacher that steam heat is hard to control in April." Then, in a different, happy voice he said, "Did you know that long, long ago, April was the first month of the year and had thirty-six days?"

Mickey shook her head.

Mr. B. went back to his stern maintenance man voice. "If I turn the boiler down very much at night, the building is too cold the next morning," he said. "If I keep it warm, the rooms on the west get too hot by afternoon. Is your classroom on the west?"

"I'm not here about the heat," Mickey said.

"Oh." He waited for her to explain.

She didn't know how to start. There was no reason Mr. B. should answer her questions.

When Mickey didn't say anything, Mr. B. picked up his book again. This time he read out loud.

"The name April probably comes from a Latin word meaning 'I open,' because tree buds and flowers begin to open in April." He smiled at her. "Isn't that interesting?"

Mickey felt more at ease. Mr. B. was just like Kate — always reading weird books. Mickey wished that her sister was here. She and Mr. B. would get along well together.

"Of course, some think the word comes from the Greek goddess Aphrodite."

"Yesterday —" Mickey began.

28

"Was the last day of the Hindu feast of Huli," said Mr. B. "Some scholars believe that's where April Fool's Day started."

"Yesterday," Mickey repeated, "what time did the lunchroom helpers finish in the kitchen?"

He put down the book again and said, "I don't remember. Four o'clock, maybe a little earlier." He thought for a moment. "Yes, it was before four. One of them had to catch the four o'clock school bus." He began to read again as if everything were settled.

When Mickey didn't leave, he looked at her over the top of the book.

"Is there some problem?" he asked. "If she missed the bus, it's not my fault. I stayed in the kitchen to lock up after them."

Another important clue, thought Mickey.

"You were in the kitchen when they left?" she asked.

"Yes. I had to be sure that everything was turned off."

So no one else could have sneaked into the kitchen. It had to be one of the student helpers. Or a friend of theirs.

Mr. B. looked worried. "It's about the snake, isn't it? I told Mr. Jacobi that I didn't see anything," he said.

Mickey said, "We just want to be sure that yesterday's helpers get credit for the time they worked."

Mr. B. said, "They signed the schedule."

"Oh, that's all right, then," Mickey said. "Do you still have it?"

"Of course not," Mr. B. said. "It's in the kitchen." Abruptly, he raised his book in front of his face. Their talk was over.

As she left Mr. B.'s office, Mickey remembered what someone had said about Tim Winston. If he was on kitchen duty yesterday, he might be the guilty one. And Suzy Kaminsky knew it.

8

What Suzy Didn't Know

Before Mickey could ask Kate what Suzy had said, Kate wanted to know what Mickey had learned.

Mickey said, "I know that you and Mr. B. could be friends."

"Why?" Kate asked.

"Because he reads strange books, too. What did you find out?"

"Suzy wasn't in the kitchen yesterday. They only work one day a week."

That probably meant that their best suspect was innocent. Tim had worked today, too.

"Who *was* there yesterday?" Mickey asked.

"Suzy didn't know," Kate said. "They switch around when someone is ill. A fourth-grade boy usually has Wednesdays. But he got the flu, so someone else filled in."

"We need Mrs. Riley's help again," Mickey said.

"Why?" asked Kate.

"I want to see who signed yesterday's kitchen schedule."

Mrs. Riley wasn't in the teachers' lounge. One of the other teachers told them that Mr. Jacobi had asked her to bring Billy Wade to the office.

Kate said, "Do you suppose Billy really did it?"

"No," Mickey said. "But someone wants us to think he did."

"Who?"

"I don't know," Mickey said. "Perhaps the real joker, who's scared of being caught. Let's see if we can get the schedule without Mrs. Riley's help."

9

Who Was in the Kitchen?

In the kitchen, Mrs. Gately was emptying salt shakers.

"We're sorry to bother you," Kate said.

Without looking up, Mrs. Gately said, "If you lost a pencil case, there's a blue one on the table in the storeroom."

Mickey said, "We came about the snake."

Mrs. Gately put down a salt shaker. She looked tired. "I remember now. You — one of you was here with Mrs. Riley." She sighed. "I'm glad that April Fool's Day is only once a year."

Kate said, "We're trying to find the guilty one."

"Billy Wade did it," Mrs. Gately said.

Mickey said, "We don't think so."

Mrs. Gately said, "Mr. Jacobi spoke to Billy's mother. She told him that Billy left very early this morning."

Kate looked at her sister uncertainly. But Mickey still seemed confident.

"Of course. He wanted us to sit on the floor. The joke wouldn't work unless he got here early enough to tell everyone."

Kate grinned. Because she'd been so late, she didn't know about sitting on the floor. But that sounded like something Billy would think up.

Mickey said, "Who was here after you left last night?"

"Let me think," Mrs. Gately said. She rubbed her forehead. "I'm still a little fuzzy. I'll have to check." She went into the back storeroom.

"Where's the flour bin?" Kate whispered.

Mickey said, "Over next to the stove."

Kate touched the metal bin.

Mrs. Gately came back with a clipboard. "Carol Clark filled in," she said. "I'm sure she didn't have a snake."

"The snake may not have been here last night," Kate said.

34

Mickey said, "You told me the snake *had* to be here all night."

"That was before I saw the kitchen. Mrs. Gately, what time did you light the oven this morning?" Kate asked.

"About seven-thirty."

"And was the flour bin next to it?"

"It's always next to the stove."

"Then someone brought in the snake just before you found it."

"But you said —" Mickey began.

"I said snakes don't have thermostats to control their body temperature. They aren't very active when it's cold." She paused. "They also slow down when they're hot. Feel the bin."

35

Mickey put her hand against the metal. "It's warm."

"With the stove on," Kate said, "it would be hot."

Mickey understood. "A hot snake wouldn't have slithered across Mrs. Gately's hand."

36

"Right," said Kate.

Mrs. Gately said, "No wonder Mr. Jacobi was able to catch it so easily after it wriggled under the stove. I thought it was awfully quiet when he pulled it out."

Mickey said, "Who came in this morning?"

"No one," Mrs. Gately said. Then she looked thoughtful. "I did hear the door open when I was taking inventory in the storeroom. I didn't remember until just this minute."

"So we still don't know who did it," Kate said.

"Maybe we do," said Mickey. "Whoever slipped in would have waited until the hallway was empty."

"But that would have made him late for class."

"Or almost late," Mickey said.

Together they said, "Angela Fergusen."

"At lunchtime, Angela was the one who was spreading the rumor that Billy Wade did it," Mickey said.

Kate said, "And her older brother has snakes as pets."

10

The Case Is Closed

Recess was over. Noisy children crowded the hall-way.

"What do we do now?" Kate asked.

Mickey said, "We find Angela."

"If she's guilty, she'll never admit it."

"Maybe she would if she knew we were going to tell Billy."

"Why would that make her confess?"

Mickey said, "Would you want Billy Wade after you?"

"I guess not," Kate said. "He's enough of a pest when he likes you."

Angela was in the hall outside their classroom. She had a smug smile on her face.

"Did you hear about Billy?" she asked.

"Yes," said Mickey. "But he didn't do it."

"What do you mean?" Angela said. "Of course he did it."

Kate said, "Where do you suppose he got a blue racer?"

"How would I know?"

Kate continued. "Garter snakes are pretty common. But I've never seen a blue racer except in the zoo."

"They're around. My brother —" Angela stopped.

"Your brother has snakes, doesn't he?" Mickey said.

"So what? That doesn't prove I put the snake in the flour bin."

Kate said, "You came in right after me this morning." She said it slowly, accenting each word.

Suddenly, Angela turned pale. "I was afraid you might have seen me coming out of the kitchen. Are you going to tell Mrs. Riley?"

"No," Kate said. "We're going to tell Billy Wade. *You're* going to tell Mrs. Riley."

"You can't make me."

Kate looked at her sister. "I wonder what Billy will do when he finds out," she said.

Suddenly, Mickey remembered something. "Yanking a jump rope away is nothing compared to what he might do."

Angela's shoulders sagged. "Even if I told Mrs. Riley, Billy would still be after me."

Mickey said, "If you get him out of trouble, he might forgive you for getting him in trouble."

Angela considered that.

"All right," she said. "I'll tell Mrs. Riley."

"And apologize to Mrs. Gately," Kate said.

Angela said, "I never meant for her to get hurt. It was just an April Fool's Day joke."

Mrs. Riley came to the door. "Are you girls coming in?"

Angela said, "May I talk to you, Mrs. Riley?"

Their teacher looked at the Dixon twins. There was a small smile on her face. Kate thought that she even saw a half wink.

"Of course," Mrs. Riley said. "Kate and Mickey, the social studies assignment is on the board."

As the twins walked into the classroom, Kate whispered, "What was that about a jump rope?"

"Billy yanked her jump rope yesterday," said Mickey. "That was her motive for trying to frame him." She handed Kate a quarter.

"The case is closed. Good job, partner."